# RASCAL'S SURPRISE PRIZE

## A Book about Kindness

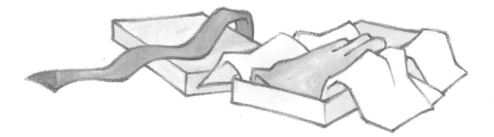

*Paula Bussard*
*Illustrated by Terry Julien*

**Chariot Books**™
David C. Cook Publishing Co.

Chariot Books™ is an imprint of David C. Cook Publishing Co.
David C. Cook Publishing Co., Elgin, Illinois 60120
David C. Cook Publishing Co., Weston, Ontario
Nova Distribution LTD., Torquay, England

RASCAL'S SURPRISE PRIZE
© 1991 by Loveland Communications for text and illustrations

Illustrated and Designed by Terry Julien
First Printing, 1991
Printed in the United States of America
95 94 93 92      5 4 3 2

Scripture quoted from the *International Children's Bible, New Century
Version*, copyright © 1986 by Sweet Publishing, Fort Worth, Texas
76137. Used by permission.

**Library of Congress Cataloging-in-Publication Data**

Bussard, Paula J.
        Rascal's surprise prize/by Paula Bussard.
                p.      cm.
        Summary: Rascal the raccoon is tempted to steal a pair of gloves
for Grandmother Mouse.
        ISBN 1-55513-942-6
[1. Shoplifting—Fiction. 2. Kindness—Fiction. 3. Christian life—
Fiction.] I. Title.
PZ7.B9658Rae   1991
[E]—dc20

                                                        91-8535
                                                        CIP
                                                        AC

Hello, my friends,

Welcome to Critter County. I have a story for you about Rascal, my favorite raccoon. He's just about your age, and he loves to play baseball!

Have you ever won a prize? In this story, Rascal wants to win a prize. You'll have to read the book (or have someone read it to you) to find out what happens to him.

When you finish the story, turn to the last page in the book, and I'll have something for you to do.

Love,

*Christine Wyrtzen*

"Hey, 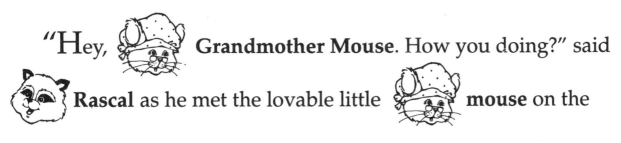 **Grandmother Mouse**. How you doing?" said **Rascal** as he met the lovable little **mouse** on the street one afternoon.

"Hello, **Rascal**. Oh, I'm pretty good. But I'm just a wee bit frustrated because I've lost one of my new **gloves.** I thought it was here in my **handbag**, but it's gone . . . lost. . . ."

"I'll keep an eye out for it. I'm on my way to a baseball game. Each time I hit a homer and run the bases, I'll look for your 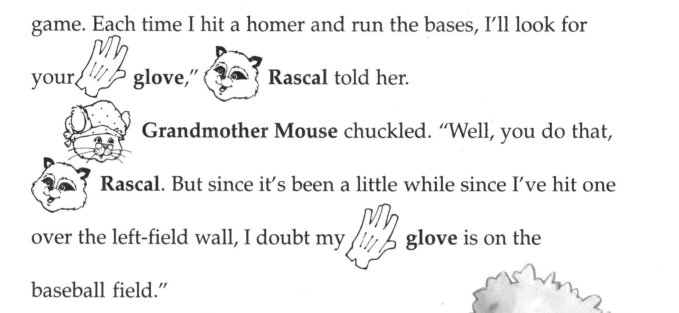 **glove**," **Rascal** told her.

**Grandmother Mouse** chuckled. "Well, you do that, **Rascal**. But since it's been a little while since I've hit one over the left-field wall, I doubt my **glove** is on the baseball field."

The next day Rascal and the other critters sat in school listening to their teacher, Mrs. Ostrich. She was explaining a new contest to the class.

"To win the trophy, you have to be the student who has done the kindest act for someone else. So use your brain power to come up with an idea that will truly touch someone's heart and make him feel loved," she said with a smile.

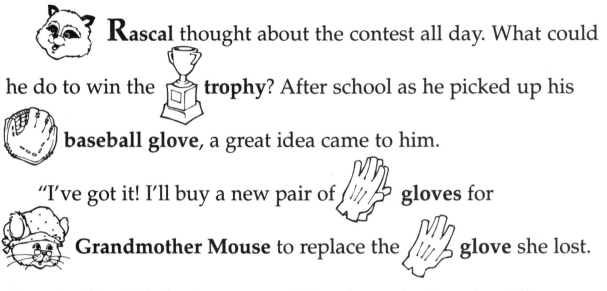

**R**ascal thought about the contest all day. What could he do to win the trophy? After school as he picked up his baseball glove, a great idea came to him.

"I've got it! I'll buy a new pair of gloves for Grandmother Mouse to replace the glove she lost.

Yes, sir, this little brainstorm will land me that trophy. I'll go home and open my piggy  **bank**. Then I'll go to the Fur and Feather Clothing **Store** to buy her a new pair of mouse **gloves**. Oh, I am going to win!" Rascal said to himself.

 **R**ascal emptied his bank all over his blue quilt. Was there enough money to buy the gloves? Rascal stuffed the money in his pocket and raced off to the store.

What a busy store! Everyone in Critter County seemed to be trying on new clothes that afternoon, and all the salespeople were busy helping them. Rascal looked around the crowd.

"No one can help me, so I will have to find the  gloves myself," Rascal decided, and he went straight to the

glove department. He flipped big gloves and

little gloves all through the air as he hunted for mouse

gloves.

Sure enough. A pair that would fit Grandmother

Mouse. He looked at the price tag. "Whew! That's going to take

all the money I've earned mowing lawns. I hope I have

enough  **money** to pay for these gloves," Rascal thought.

Just then, a terrible idea came to Rascal. *Would anyone miss the gloves if I just took them?*

**Rascal** looked around. Everyone was busy. No one had even noticed him come into the **store**. . . . "I know I could stick these **gloves** in my pocket and not get caught," he thought.

"Wait a minute! What in the world am I thinking? What am I using for brains? **Spaghetti**? I can't steal **gloves**," he told himself. "That would be wrong. The contest is to show kindness to someone else. The **trophy** will be won by the critter who helps make someone else happy. Oh, **Rascal**, steal the **gloves**? Where are your brains?"

 **R**ascal took the gloves off the shelf and went to the salesclerk, Liona Lou. "Pardon me, ma'am," he said politely. "I want to buy these gloves for Grandmother Mouse. She lost one of her gloves."

"Why, Rascal, what a wonderful idea. As my tail does wag, these gloves are just like the ones I sold Grandmother Mouse last week!" exclaimed Liona Lou. "Why, she'll swing from the streetlights by her tail when she sees this gift."

**R**ascal dug the money out of his pocket.

"Here's my lawn-mowing money. I think it's enough. It's all I have," he said, handing Liona Lou the money.

"**Rascal**, that's just the right amount. Let me wrap the gloves for you," Liona Lou said.

As 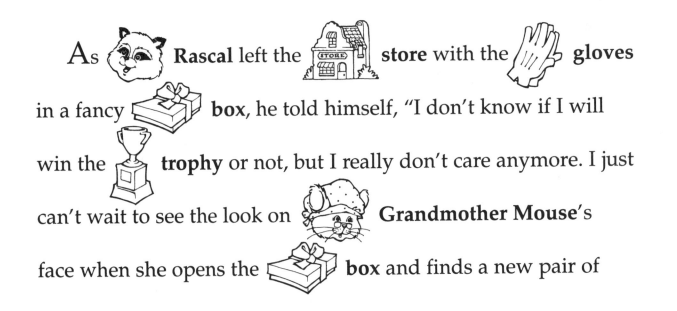 **Rascal** left the **store** with the **gloves** in a fancy **box**, he told himself, "I don't know if I will win the **trophy** or not, but I really don't care anymore. I just can't wait to see the look on **Grandmother Mouse**'s face when she opens the **box** and finds a new pair of

 **gloves**. I just can't wait! Um, I wonder if she'd laugh if I told her I found them on the baseball field as I was running the bases?"

Hi again, kids,

What do you think Rascal learned about being kind and loving? Why didn't he care if he won the trophy? How do you think Grandmother Mouse felt when Rascal gave her the new gloves?

You know, God wants us to be kind to others. God's Word says, "Be kind and loving to each other" (Ephesians 4:32a). What are some ways you can be kind and loving to someone this week?

After you've done something kind, would you write to me and Rascal and tell us about it? Also, in your letter, be sure to praise Rascal for buying the gloves for Grandmother Mouse. That will encourage him to be kind in the future.

Thanks for visiting Critter County. I hope you'll enjoy our other books and tapes about your Critter County friends. And why don't you write to Rascal right now?

Love,
*Christine Wyrtzen*

Write to: Rascal, Critter County, Box 8, Loveland, Ohio 45140